Aladdin Books
Macmillan Publishing Company
866 Third Avenue, New York, NY 10022
Collier Macmillan Canada, Inc.
First Aladdin Books edition 1988
Printed in Italy

10   9   8   7   6   5   4   3   2   1

Library of Congress Cataloging-in-Publication Data
Tenaille, Marie.
The robot on vacation.
(Aladdin storybooks)
Translation of: Un robot pour les vacances.
Summary: Charlie, a tiny robot who can do everything,
runs away from the professor who made him and joins
a human family on their vacation.
[1. Robots – Fiction] 2. Vacations – Fiction]
I. Touvay, Monique, ill. II. Title. III. Series.
PZ7.T2632Ro 1988   [E]   88-16743
ISBN 0-689-71280-4

The Robot on Vacation

by Marie Tenaille

illustrated by Monique Touvay

translation from the French
by Didi Charney

"Hi, my name is Charlie!"

Aladdin Books
Macmillan Publishing Company
New York

Professor Nicholas had been waiting for this moment for years. Today was the day that he would test his special miniature robot!

"Your name is Charles," he said to the robot. "You can talk, listen, think—you can do everything that I do, Charles."

"Okay!" chirped the robot in a little metallic voice. "But can you call me Charlie?"

"Charlie..." said the professor slowly. "You're really talking! I can't believe this. ...Charlie," he continued, "today I'd like to give you a test run."

"I want to make sure that you work perfectly before I go on vacation tomorrow. Now let's begin. Please go to the garden and pick me some flowers."

At the word *vacation*, a little click went off in Charlie's head. He moved jerkily toward the front door. And then, more quickly, he opened it and walked out.

But not toward the garden! Instead, he walked toward the gate, opened the latch, and went off—on his own vacation.

Poor Professor Nicholas didn't even hear the gate slam shut.

Words like *vacation, trip, car,* and
adventure spun around in Charlie's head.

12

The first thing he saw was a highway, so he began to follow it.

Soon he saw a gas station. Just as he got there, a bright red car stopped to get some gas. So Charlie stuck his thumb out.

"Look! There's a robot – hitchhiking!" cried the three children in the backseat. They quickly called to Charlie, "Get in before anyone else sees you."

Charlie jumped in and hid himself between them.

"Ouch!" howled Tommy, the youngest. "You're squishing me!" Alex and Susan quickly shushed him.

"Settle down," ordered their father, who was just getting back into the car. No one saw Charlie...and the only thing the children's parents heard from the backseat was whispering. Alex, Susan, and Tommy were asking Charlie all sorts of questions.

"This is great!" Alex said. "Let's fool Mom and Dad."

"Mom, ask us some questions," said Susan.

"Who is buried in Grant's Tomb?" their mother asked.

"Lincoln," whispered Charlie to Tommy, who said the answer out loud.

Everyone laughed, but that didn't bother Charlie.

"How tall is the Empire State Building?" asked their father.

"0521 feet," Charlie told Susan. And when she said it, everyone laughed again.

"That's strange," said their father. "You said it backward."

"Mount Everest's altitude? The year of the Revolutionary War?" asked Mom.

"82,092 feet! 6771!" chirped the tiny metallic voice.

But no one heard the answers, because their father was saying, "We're here! Alex, Susan, and Tommy—please take the things out of the car while we open up the house."

"Can you stay in the car so our parents don't see you?" Alex asked Charlie.

"Okay," said Charlie. "But I want to help!"

"What a funny robot!" exclaimed Susan.

"I think he's a little crazy," Alex said. "He gets everything wrong."

"I like him just the way he is," Tommy declared stubbornly.

So Charlie sat in the backseat, watching them through the window. "I want to help," he repeated.

And before they knew it, he'd hurried
out onto the driveway ... and started
reloading the car! He was so fast that none
of the children could stop him.

"A robot for the house!" cried their
parents. "Just the kind of help we need!"

At that, Charlie turned and walked away
as fast as he could. He was so upset at
being called a servant that all of his alarms
went off.

"No, Mom—no, Dad!" the children shouted. "He's not like that. He's our *friend*. We saw him at the gas station, and—"

"What does he know how to do?" asked their father.

"Everything!" they replied. "He knows everything, he can do everything, but ..."

Their mother and father thought that Charlie was great. They had a long talk with him while the children watched. Charlie seemed to like their parents, which made the children a little jealous.

"Pretty soon he'll be shining Dad's shoes instead of making us jelly sandwiches," groaned Alex. "Charlie, we're starving!"

But Charlie did everything—almost. Their father's shoes were covered with jelly, and their sandwiches were shined and polished!

After the children had stopped laughing, Charlie explained: "You've got to ask me to do only one thing at a time." He was a little embarrassed. "That's how I'm made."

Everyone in the neighborhood came over to have a look at the robot.

"Isn't he cute!"

"Where'd you find him?"

"Can you talk to him?"

"What does he do?"

"Everything!" beamed Charlie. The children just smiled.

"Charlie," said their mother, "please

serve our guests now, so they can see what you can do."

This time, he did everything right. Alex, Susan, and Tommy were a little annoyed at that.

"It's time to water the flowers, Charlie," they said, giggling.

Charlie picked up the hose, turned it on, and sprayed all of the neighbors! They left right away—which was just what the children wanted!

Then the four of them sat down in the
living room to watch TV. There was a
special news bulletin on—Professor
Nicholas was in the middle of making an
important announcement.

"My robot, Charlie, escaped before I could test him. He knows how to do everything, but there might still be a screw loose somewhere. If you see him, please send him back to me."

The only thing to do was to send Charlie home ... even though the children didn't want to.

"Do you recognize this road?" asked
Susan. "Think hard."

"Sure," said Charlie. They all hoped he
was right.

And for once, he was! The gate was
unlocked, just as he'd left it, and the

professor was waiting at the front door.
Charlie couldn't wait to tell him everything.

On their next vacation, Alex, Susan, and Tommy are going to visit *Charlie*.

And none of them can wait!

33

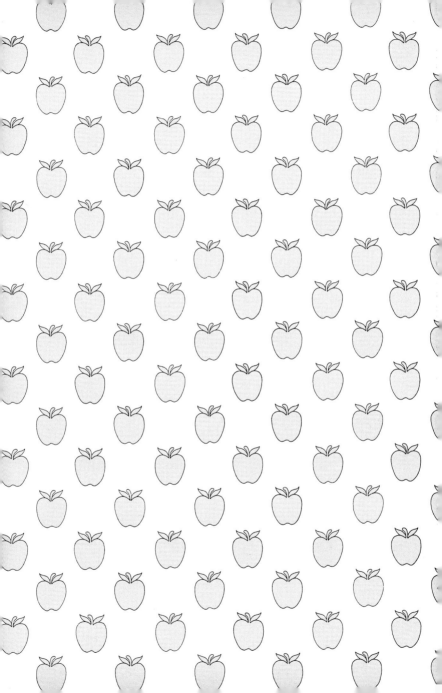